First American Edition 2018
Kane Miller, A Division of EDC Publishing

Copyright © 2015 by Courtney Dicmas
First published in the UK in 2015 by Templar Publishing, part of the Bonnier Publishing Group

All rights reserved

For information contact:
Kane Miller, A Division of EDC Publishing
www.kanemiller.com

Library of Congress Control Number: 2017947142

Printed in Malaysia
1 2 3 4 5 6 7 8 9 10

For Martin, Pam and Jin Cho Youn

LeMUR DREAMER

Courtney Dicmas

Kane Miller
A DIVISION OF EDC PUBLISHING

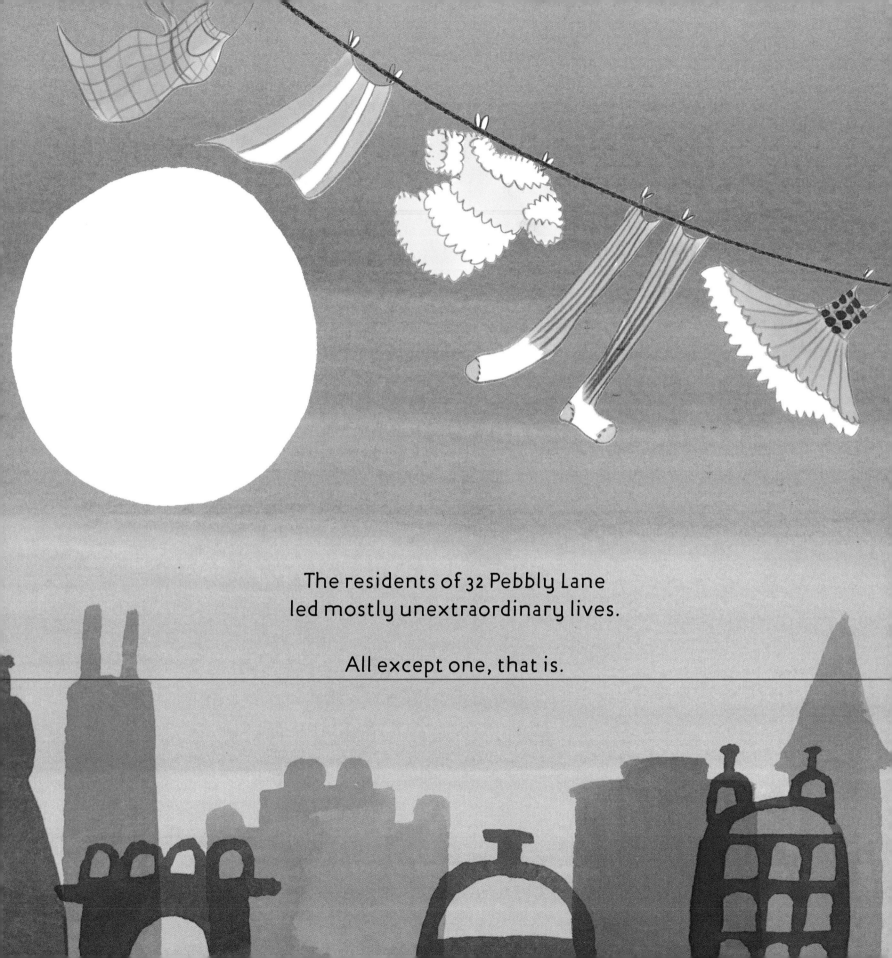

The residents of 32 Pebbly Lane
led mostly unextraordinary lives.

All except one, that is.

Louis, who lived on
the very top floor,

had the unfortunate habit...

of **sleepwalking!**

Every night, fast asleep, Louis wandered out his front door, snoozed around the other apartments, and snuffled back to bed.

Z Z Z Z Z Z Z Z

It wasn't a problem at first.

The neighbors were very understanding.

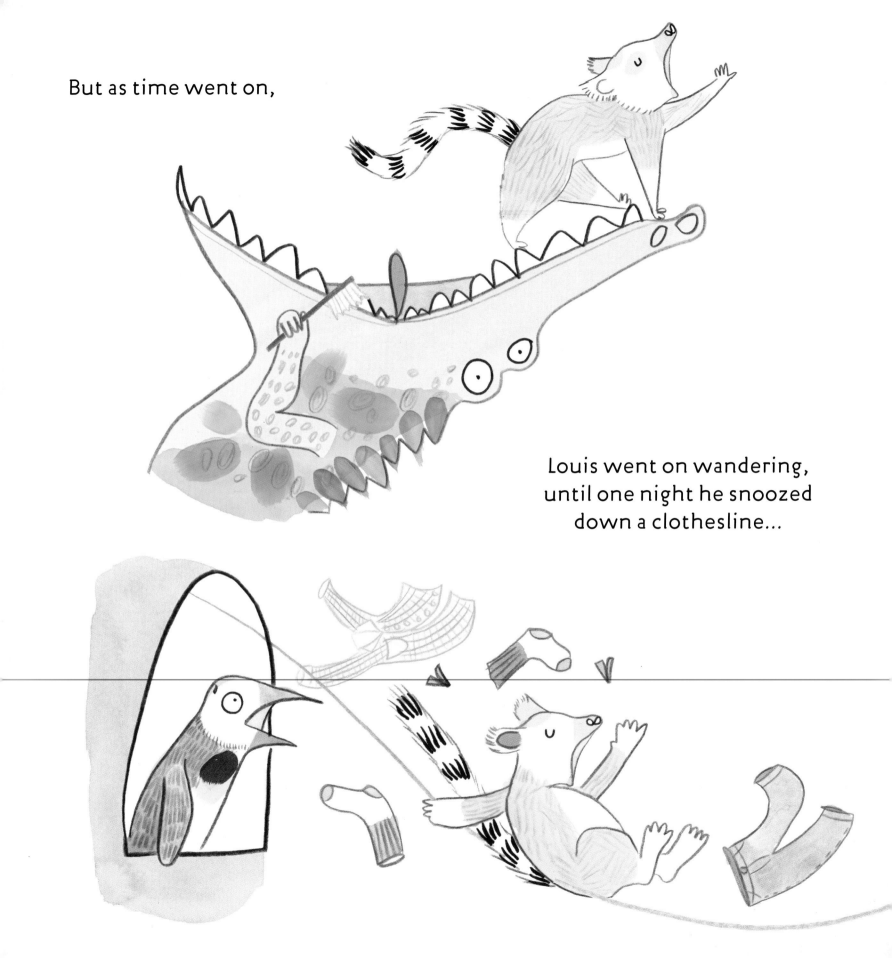

But as time went on,

Louis went on wandering,
until one night he snoozed
down a clothesline...

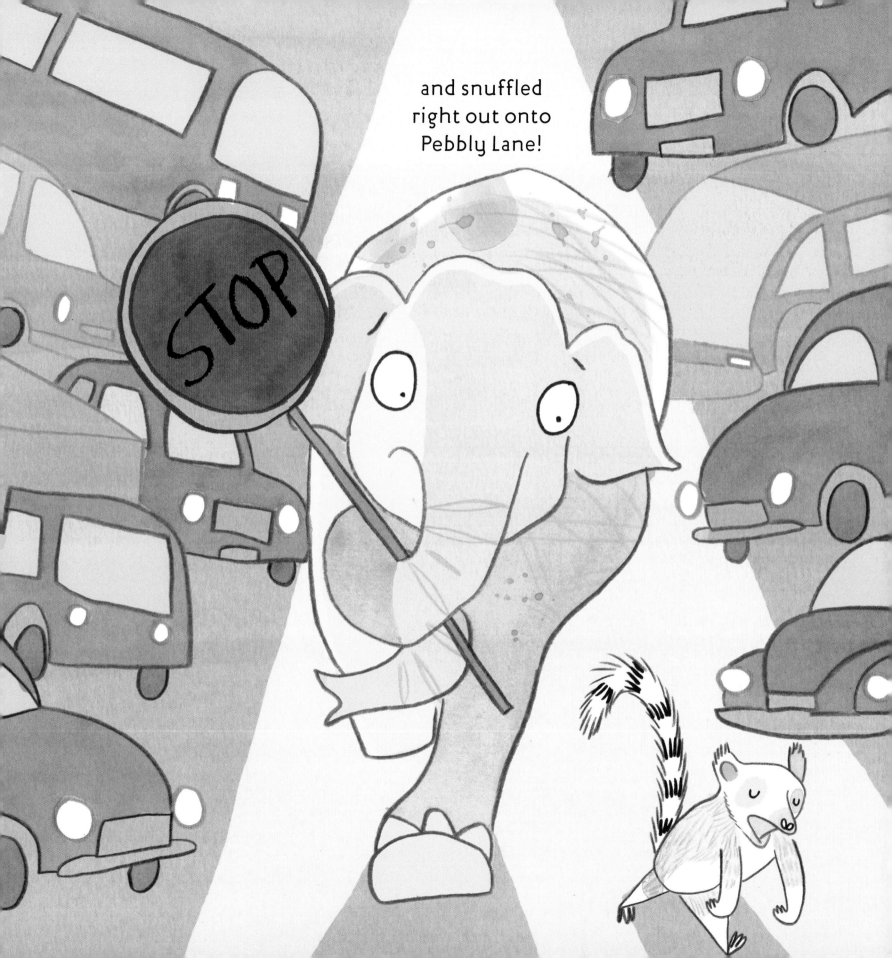

and snuffled
right out onto
Pebbly Lane!

sssh

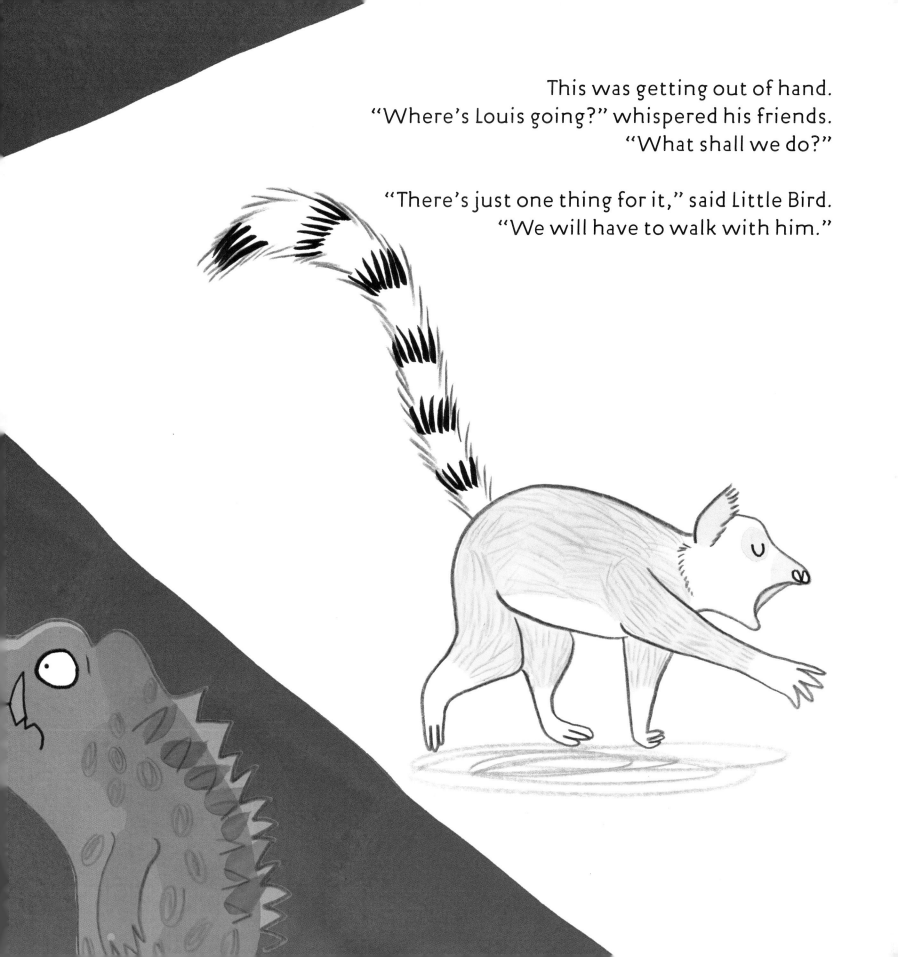

This was getting out of hand.
"Where's Louis going?" whispered his friends.
"What shall we do?"

"There's just one thing for it," said Little Bird.
"We will have to walk with him."

So as Louis snored beyond Pebbly Lane, his friends tiptoed close behind.

No one knew what he was dreaming of.

But whatever it was...

and wherever he went...

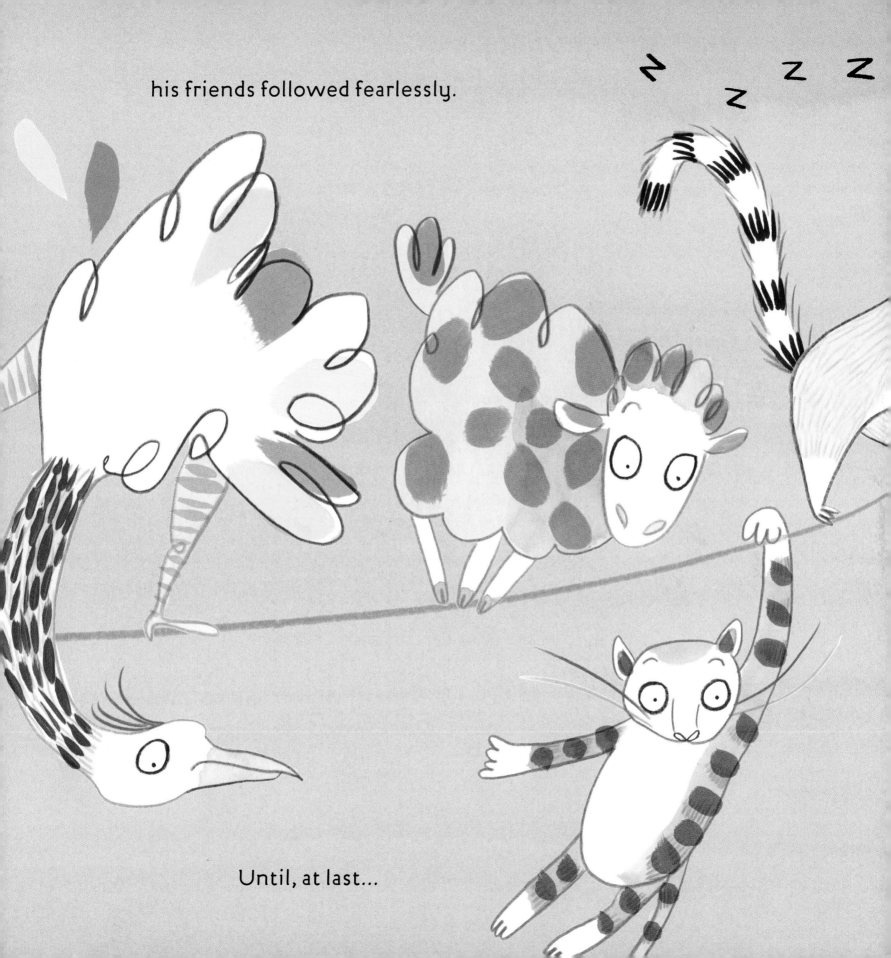

his friends followed fearlessly.

Until, at last...

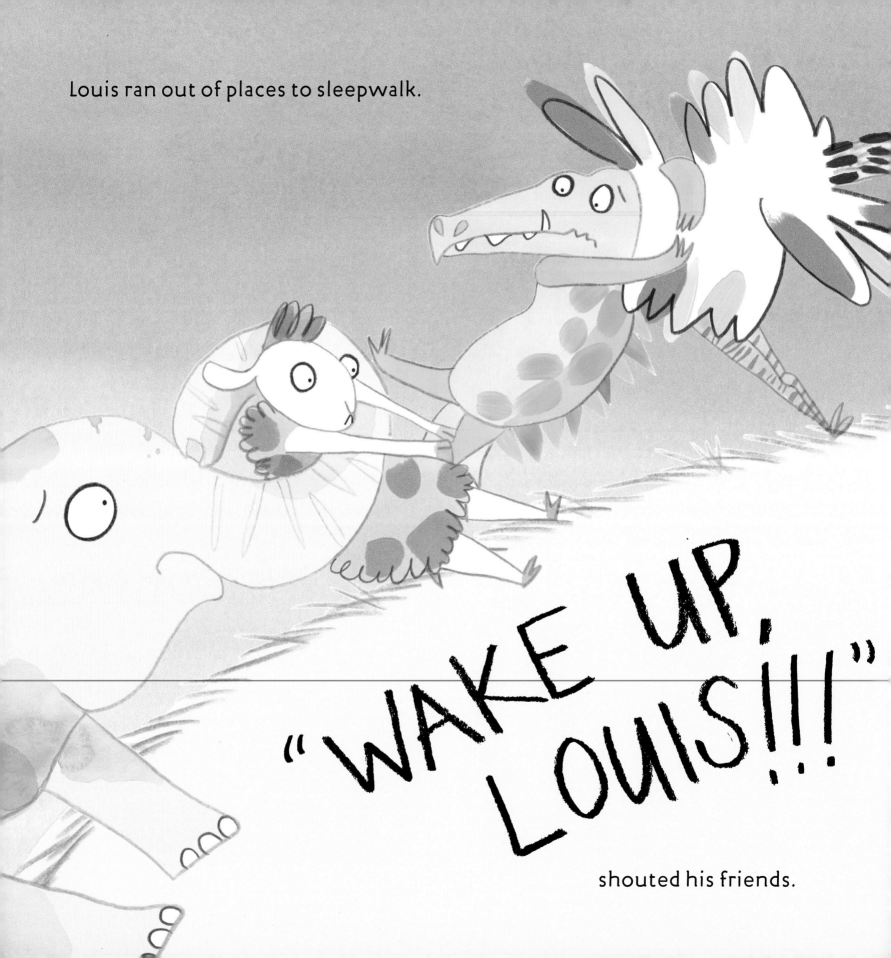

Louis ran out of places to sleepwalk.

"WAKE UP, LOUIS!!!"

shouted his friends.

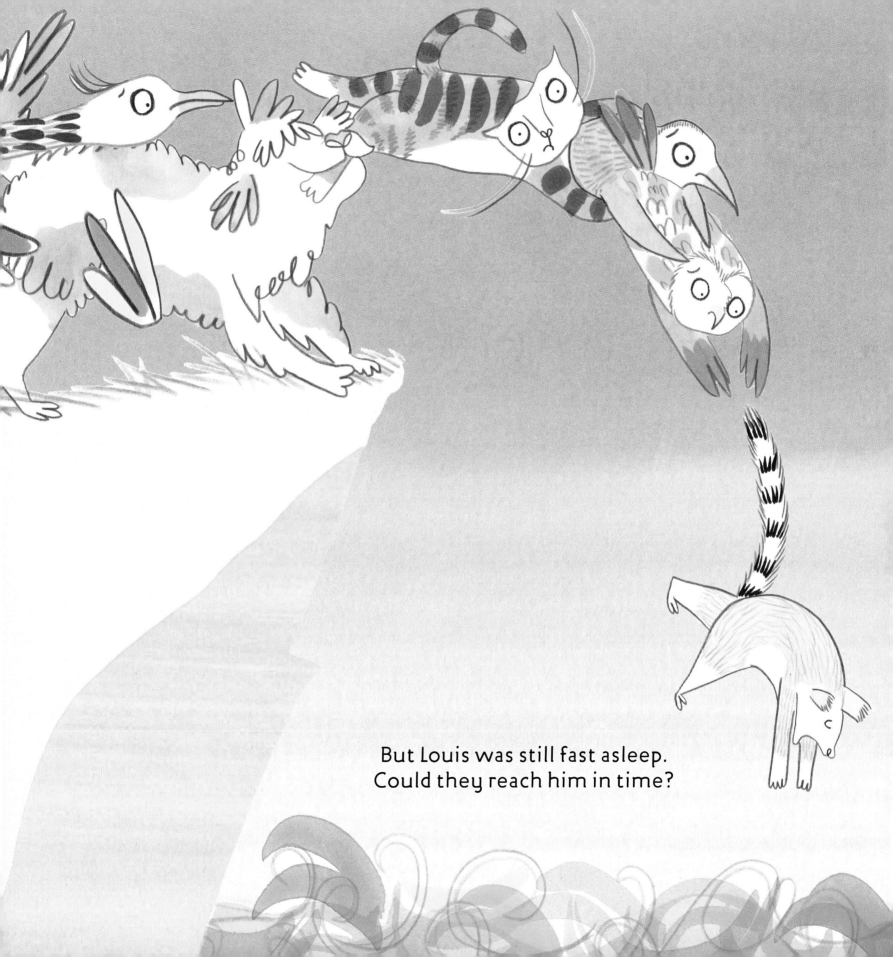

But Louis was still fast asleep.
Could they reach him in time?

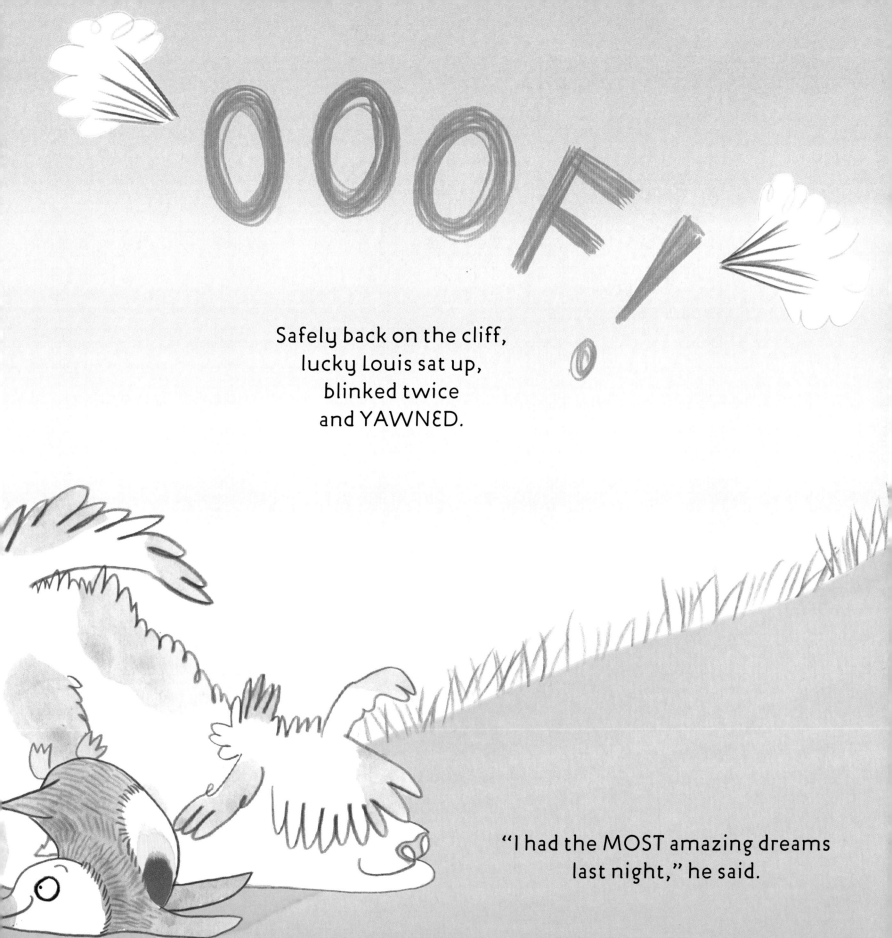

OOOF!

Safely back on the cliff,
lucky Louis sat up,
blinked twice
and YAWNED.

"I had the MOST amazing dreams
last night," he said.

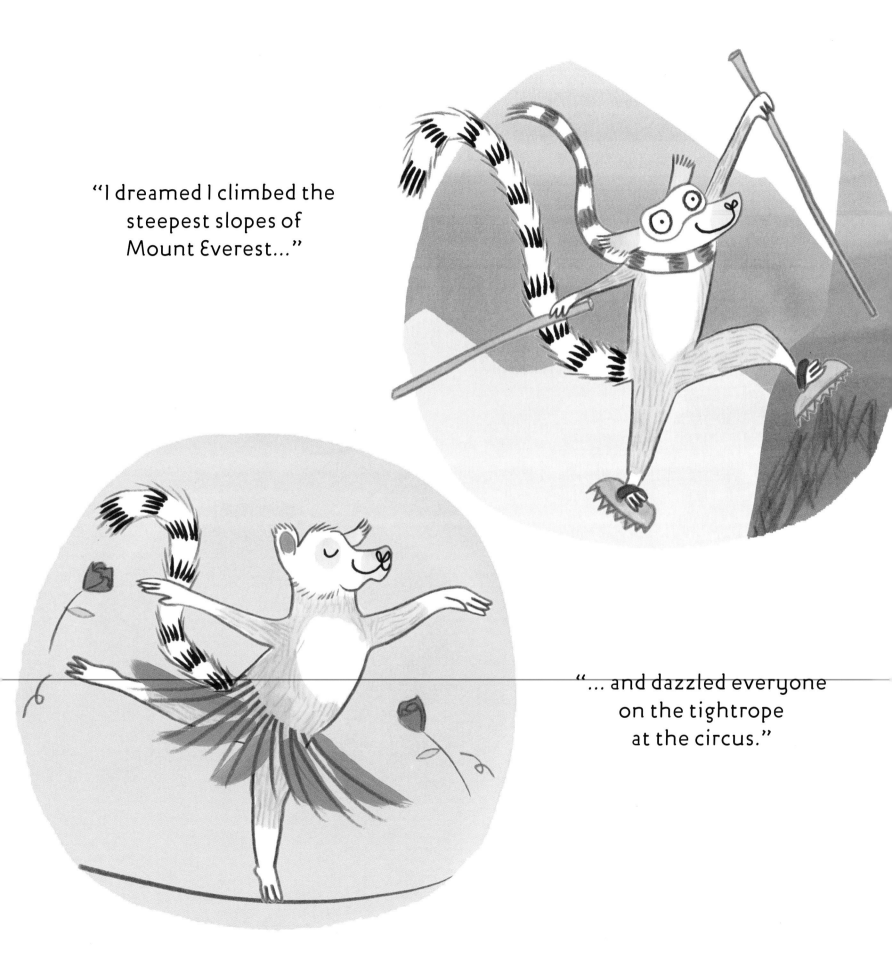

"I dreamed I climbed the steepest slopes of Mount Everest..."

"... and dazzled everyone on the tightrope at the circus."

"Then, I was just about to go scuba diving on the Great Barrier Reef, when something stopped me."

"But where am I? And what are you all doing here?

Hold on a minute..."

"I've been sleepwalking again!"

Louis felt terrible. He'd caused his friends so much trouble.
But they didn't mind. They loved Louis, even with all his snoozing and snuffling.

So to cheer him up, the next day
his friends decided to get Louis
a special present.

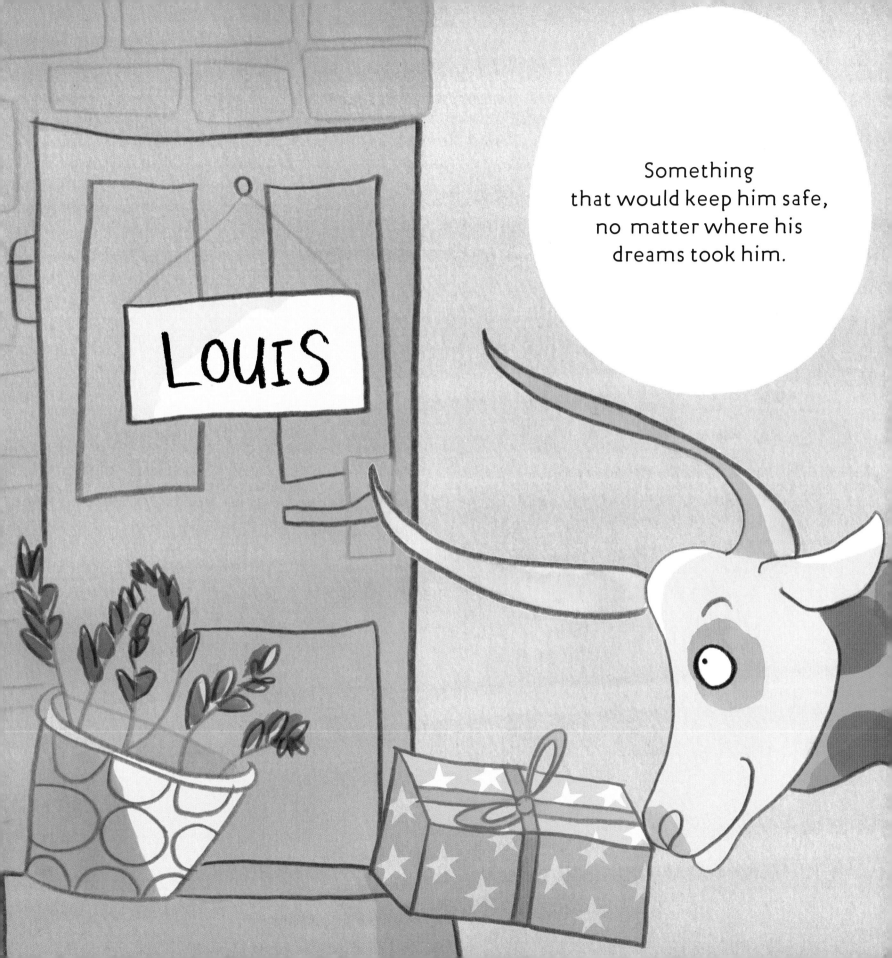

Something
that would keep him safe,
no matter where his
dreams took him.

Because that's what friends are for.